JFK

Jonah Winter   illustrated by AG Ford

KATHERINE TEGEN BOOKS
An Imprint of HarperCollins Publishers

For Gunnel Ragner —Jonah Winter

To my lovely wife, Brandy —AG Ford

Katherine Tegen Books is an imprint of HarperCollins Publishers.

JFK
Text copyright © 2013 by Jonah Winter
Illustrations copyright © 2013 by AG Ford

Library of Congress Cataloging-in-Publication Data is available.
ISBN 978-0-06-176807-1

Typography by Rachel Zegar
13 14 15 16 17   SCP   10 9 8 7 6 5 4 3 2 1
❖
First Edition

Once upon a time in America, there was a man who mattered to a lot of people. His name was John F. Kennedy. He was president when I was born in 1962.

I saw him once. It was in Dallas, Texas. I was only one year old, too young to understand what I was seeing. Sitting on my father's shoulders, though,

I watched his car pass by, watched him waving to the crowds of cheering people, watched him getting smaller and smaller as the car drove on.

We left the parade early and went to a friend's house. She was in tears. "Someone shot the president!" she said. Minutes later, that same day, President John F. Kennedy was dead.

I've heard this story so many times. People all over the country and all over the world were staring at their televisions, horrified,

crying. *How could this have happened? And why?* These are questions people still ask.

But this isn't just a story of sadness and death. It's a story of hope and courage. It's a story about the power of words. It's a story that begins before the birth of John Fitzgerald Kennedy.

It begins on the boat that carried his great-grandparents all the way from their home in Ireland to the shores of America, in search of a better life.

It's a story that could not have happened without the ambition of John's father, who shrugged off American prejudice against his Irish roots as he made his fortune.

And it's a story of how Kennedy's Irish Catholic family was destined to be among the most powerful families in American history.

Joe Jr. was the oldest son, and his parents dreamed that he might someday be president. He was smart. He was responsible. He was ambitious.

John, the second oldest, was often sick, and no one expected much from him. He was a daydreamer. He loved to lie in bed and read. He loved words.

One of his favorite books was about King Arthur, the good, wise king of English legend. This was young John Kennedy's hero—a fearless leader, beloved of his people, who ruled from his mythical castle named Camelot.

John also looked up to his older brother, though he couldn't help but compete. They loved to wrestle and sometimes even fought, as brothers often do in childhood.

But childhood ended. And World War II began. And both brothers enlisted to fight in the war.

John came home a hero. When his torpedo boat was sunk, he saved one of his men from drowning, swimming with the man draped across his back, which would always be in pain from this day on.

Joe was not so lucky. His plane went down over England. And suddenly the perfect son, the highest hope for the Kennedy family, was dead.

Slowly, the Kennedy family's dream—the greatest of all American dreams, *the presidency*—was shifted onto John. John was not so sure he wanted such a life. He loved to read, and he loved to write. Words were what he loved.

But he also believed in public service. It was why he had fought in the war. And that was also why, with help from his father, he decided to go into politics. And much to his father's delight, John was a natural! He charmed every person he met. And as a very young man, he was elected to the U.S. Senate.

As a senator, though, he didn't stop writing. In fact, he wrote a prizewinning book called *Profiles in Courage*. It was about eight great senators who had stood up for what they believed in, even when it cost them popularity. You could see from this book what mattered most to John and how seriously he took his job.

But as we know, John F. Kennedy was destined to be more than just a senator. He knew it too. There were all sorts of things he wanted to accomplish and ways in which he would serve his country. And to do these things, he would need more power than a senator has. In 1960, with his father's help, he decided to run for president.

At first it seemed like a long shot. He was too young. He was too Catholic, and there'd never been a Catholic president. And he had this thick Boston accent, which didn't go over so well with some people. He was rich—and privileged.

Campaigning in West Virginia, he was asked how he could possibly understand the problems of working people—*had he ever done an honest day's work in his life?* "No, I can't say that I have," he responded with a chuckle—and right away, he won these people over with his honesty and charm.

John F. Kennedy had what is called "charisma," the power to inspire and excite people. All over America, John excited young people, especially—with the sound of his voice, with the words that he spoke.

He spoke with passion about America, about the world, about his dreams. His speeches were like nothing anyone had ever heard. But, truth be told, it was more than just his words that won people over. It was how he carried himself. It was his looks.

During the first-ever televised presidential debate, Kennedy looked young and fresh and presidential. His rival, Richard M. Nixon, was sick—he looked pale, sweaty, and unshaven.

Nixon had been vice president for eight years under a very popular president. He was smart and respected and much more experienced than Kennedy. Many people thought he would win. But Nixon didn't have Kennedy's charisma. Nixon didn't have Kennedy's way with words. And Nixon didn't win the election.

Kennedy's victory was not just a victory for himself but a victory for words! For intelligence! It was exciting to have such a well-spoken president. During his inauguration speech, President Kennedy said things that are still being quoted, words that are still ringing out on recordings. In his unmistakable voice he said, "Ask not what your country can do for you—ask what you can do for your country."

Patriotism, for John F. Kennedy, did not just mean waving a flag. It meant standing up for the ideals upon which our nation was founded. It meant honoring the words in the Declaration of Independence, "All men are created equal." And so, when people known as the Freedom Fighters marched through the South, protesting the unfair laws against African Americans, Kennedy sent out federal marshals to protect them.

And when Alabama governor George Wallace blocked the doors of the University of Alabama, attempting to keep out the school's first African American student, President Kennedy again sent out federal marshals to make sure that the student was allowed to go to school. He was smart about it, though. Instead of creating a fight with the governor at the entrance—which would have caused riots—Kennedy had the student taken to her dormitory. And in this instant, Kennedy brought us progress, brought us change—with a courageous act that cost him popularity in the South.

But his greatest moment as our president involved one of the scariest moments in the world's history: the Cuban Missile Crisis. The Soviet Union had moved several nuclear missiles to Cuba, an island country not far from Florida. And those missiles were pointed straight at America.

As president, he had to make a decision—to go to war or not. With his generals all advising him to bomb Cuba, to go to war, President Kennedy held back. If America went to war, the Soviets would most certainly strike back with nuclear bombs, destroying major cities, killing millions and millions of Americans.

With even his own brother—Attorney General Robert F. Kennedy—at one point advising him to go to war, President Kennedy still held back. The fate of America lay heavily on his shoulders. The clock was ticking.

The decision he made saved millions of lives. He sent America's ambassador to the United Nations, an organization formed to create world peace. And instead of declaring war, the American ambassador challenged the Soviet ambassador about the missiles. With the whole world watching, the Soviet Union backed down, removed the missiles. The crisis was over, and all without a single bomb being dropped—*just words*.

But even after the crisis was over, America and the Soviet Union were both still testing nuclear bombs—polluting the air, endangering lives, and scaring everybody. So President Kennedy signed a treaty not to blow up any more bombs aboveground. "Mankind must put an end to war," he said, "or war will put an end to mankind."

There are many more good things JFK did during his all-too-brief time as president—enough to fill many books. But he was not a perfect man, nor a perfect president. He made mistakes. He had enemies. Some even hated him—because of what he stood for, because of his wealth.

But even more people loved him—for his intelligence, his courage, his voice. He gave people hope for a better future, the same hope his Irish great-grandparents once had when they came to America.

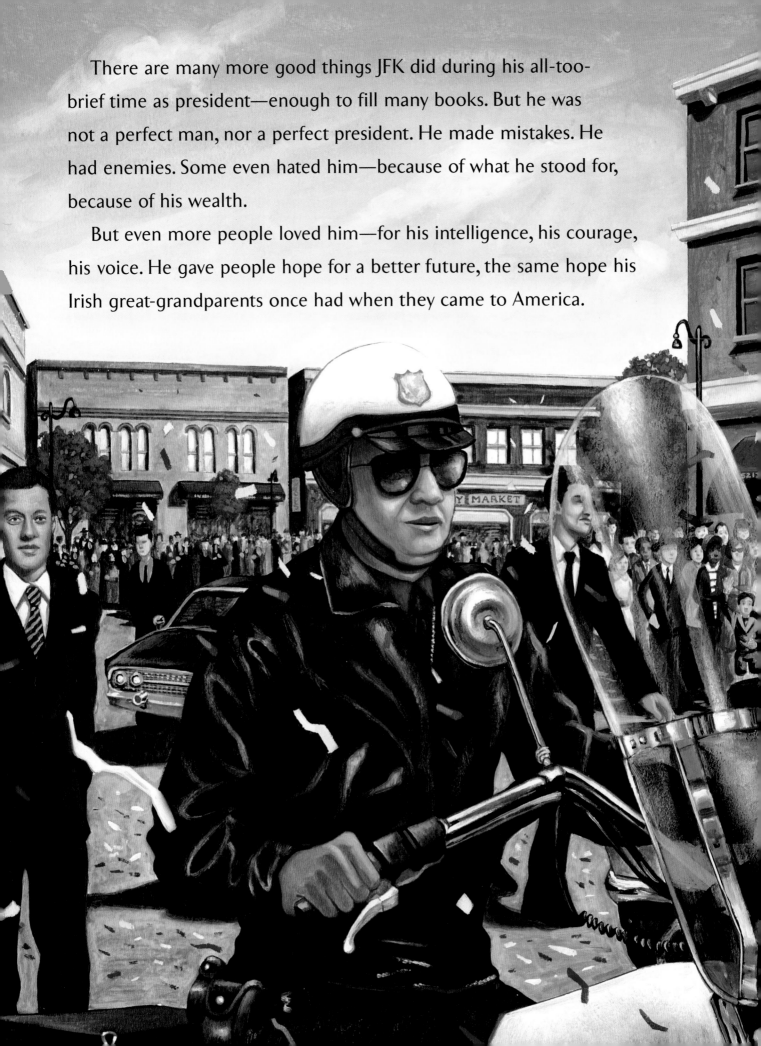

Though he was often sick and often in pain, President Kennedy never let the world see this. What the world saw was a picture of health and happiness—a smiling father sailing with his family on the open sea, a beautiful wife, adorable children, glittering parties at the White House. It was the closest America ever came to having royalty, and it is still called Camelot.

I wonder if John ever guessed, as a little boy reading the book about Camelot, what he would become to so many Americans— the hope and the excitement he would bring. I wonder if he ever guessed how much his words would someday matter. When I feel sad about his death, this is what I try to remember—for his words and his spirit live on. And that can never, ever, ever be destroyed.